SOUM

BOOKS BY AMOS OZ

FICTION

Where the Jackals Howl
Elsewhere, Perhaps
My Michael
Unto Death
Touch the Water, Touch the Wind
The Hill of Evil Counsel
A Perfect Peace
Black Box
To Know a Woman
Fima
Don't Call It Night
The Same Sea
Rhyming Life and Death

NONFICTION

In the Land of Israel
Israel, Palestine and Peace
Under This Blazing Light
The Slopes of Lebanon
The Story Begins
A Tale of Love and Darkness
How to Cure a Fanatic

FOR CHILDREN

Soumchi
Panther in the Basement
Suddenly in the Depths of the Forest

SOUMCHI

Amos Oz

TRANSLATED BY Amos Oz and Penelope Farmer

ILLUSTRATED BY Quint Buchholz

MARINER BOOKS
HOUGHTON MIFFLIN HARCOURT
Boston • New York
2012

First Mariner Books edition 2012

www.hmhbooks.com

Library of Congress Cataloging-in-Publication Data
Oz, Amos.
[Sumkhi. English]
Soumchi / Amos Oz; translated by Amos Oz and Penelope Farmer;
illustrated by Quint Buchholz. — 1st Mariner Books ed.
p. cm.
ISBN 978-0-547-63693-1
[1. Jerusalem — Fiction.] I. Farmer, Penelope, date. ill.
II. Buchholz, Quint. III. Title.
PZ7.O984So 2012
[Fic] — dc23 2012016430

Printed in the United States of America
DOC 10 9 8 7 6 5 4 3 2 1

To Fania, Gallia and Daniel

SOUMCHI

PROLOGUE

On Changes

In which may be found a variety of memories and reflections, comparisons and conclusions. You may skip them if you'd rather and pass straight on to Chapter One where my story proper begins.

Everything changes. My friends and acquaintances, for example, change curtains and professions, exchange old homes for new ones, shares for securities, or vice versa, bicycles for motor bicycles, motor bicycles for cars, exchange stamps, coins, letters, good mornings, ideas and opinions: some of them exchange smiles.

In the part of Jerusalem known as Sha'are Hesed there once lived a bank cashier who, in the course of a single month, changed his home, his wife, his appearance (he grew a red moustache and sideburns—also reddish), changed first name and surname, changed sleeping and eating habits; in short, he changed everything. One fine day he even changed his job, became a drummer in a night club instead of a cashier (though actually this was not so much a case of change, more like a sock being turned inside out).

Even while we are reflecting on it, by the way, the world about us is gradually changing too. Though the blue transparency of summer still lies across the land, though it is still hot and the sky still blazes above our heads, yet already, near dusk, you can sense some new coolness—at night comes a breeze and the smell of clouds. And just as the leaves begin to redden and to turn, so the sea becomes a little more blue, the earth a little more brown, even the far-off hills these days look somewhat farther away.

Everything.

As for me; aged eleven and two months, approximately, I changed completely, four or five times, in the course of a single day. How then shall I begin my story? With Uncle Zemach or Esthie? Either would do. But I think I'll begin with Esthie.

In Which Love Blossoms

And in which facts will at last be revealed that have been kept secret to this day; love and other feelings among them.

Near us in Zachariah Street lived a girl called Esthie. I loved her. In the morning, sitting at the breakfast table and eating a slice of bread, I'd whisper to myself, "Esthie."

To which my father would return: "One doesn't eat with one's mouth open."

While, in the evenings, they'd say of me: "That crazy boy has shut himself in the bathroom again and is playing with water."

Only I was not playing with water at all, merely filling up the hand basin and tracing her name with my finger across the waves on its surface. At night sometimes I dreamed that Esthie was pointing at me in the street, shouting, "Thief, thief!" And I would be frightened and begin to run away and she would pursue me; everyone would pursue me, Bar-Kochba Sochobolski and Goel Germanski and Aldo and Elie Weingarten, everyone, the pursuit continuing across empty lots and backyards, over fences and heaps of rusty junk, among ruins and down alleyways, until my pursuers began to grow tired and gradually to lag behind, and at last only Esthie and I would be left running all alone, reaching almost together some remote and distant spot, a woodshed, perhaps, or a washhouse on a roof, or the dark angle under the stairs of a strange house, and then the dream would become both sweet and terrible—oh, I'd awake at night sometimes and weep, almost, from shame. I wrote two love poems in the black notebook that I lost in the Tel Arza wood. Perhaps it was a good thing I lost it.

But what did Esthie know?

Esthie knew nothing. Or knew and wondered.

For example: once I put my hand up in a geography lesson and stated authoritatively:

"Lake Hula is also known as Lake Soumchi." The whole classroom of course immediately roared with loud and unruly laughter. What I had said was the truth; the exact truth in fact, it's in the encyclopedia. In spite of which, our teacher, Mr. Shitrit, got confused for a moment and interrogated me furiously: "Kindly sum up the evidence by which you support your conclusion." But the class had already erupted, was shouting and screaming from every direction:

"Sum it up, Soumchi, sum it up, Soumchi." While Mr. Shitrit swelled like a frog, grew red in the face and roared as usual:

"Let all flesh be silent!" And then, besides: "Not a dog shall bark!"

After five more minutes the class had quieted down again. But, almost to the end of the eighth grade, I remained Soumchi. I've no ulterior motive in telling you all this. I simply want to stress one significant detail; a note sent to me by Esthie at the end of that same lesson, which read as follows:

You're nuts. Why do you always have to say things that get you into trouble? Stop it!

Only then she had folded over one corner at the bottom of the note and written in it, very small: *But it doesn't matter. E.*

So what did Esthie know?

Esthie knew nothing, or perhaps she knew and wondered. As for me, in no circumstance would it have occurred to me to hide a love letter in her satchel as Elie Weingarten did in Nourit's, nor to send her a message via Ra'anana, our class matchmaker, like Tarzan Bamberger, also to Nourit. Quite the reverse: this is what I did; on every possible occasion I'd pull Esthie's plaits; time and again I stuck her beautiful white jumper to her chair with chewing gum.

Why did I do it? Because. Why not? To show her. And I'd twist her two thin arms behind her back nearly as hard as I could, until she started calling me names and trying to scratch me, yet she never begged for mercy. That's what I did to Esthie. And worse besides. It was me who first nick-named her Clementine (from the song that the English soldiers at the Schneller Barracks were spreading round Jerusalem those days: *"Oh my darling, oh my darling, oh my dar-ling Clementine!"*—the girls in our class, surprisingly, picked it up quite gleefully, and even at Hanukah six months later, when everything was over, they were still calling Esthie Tina, which came from Clementina, which came from Clementine).

And Esthie? She had only one word for me and she threw it in my face first thing every morning, before I had even had time to start making a nuisance of myself:

"Louse"—or else:

"You stink."

Once or twice at the ten o'clock break I very nearly re-duced Esthie to tears. For that I was handed punishments by Hemda, our teacher, and took them like a man, tight-lipped and uncomplaining.

And that's how love blossomed, without notable event, until the day after the feast of Shavuot. Esthie wept on my account at the ten o'clock break and I wept on hers at night.

With All His Heart and Soul

In which Uncle Zemach goes too far and I set out for the source of the River Zambezi (in the heart of Africa).

At the feast of Shavuot, Uncle Zemach came from Tel Aviv, bringing me a bicycle as a present. As a matter of fact my birthday falls between the two festivals—of Passover and Shavuot. But in Uncle Zemach's eyes, all festivals are more or less the same, except for the Tree Planting festival which he treats with exceptional respect. He used to say, "At Hanukah we children of Israel are taught in school to be angry with the wicked Greeks. At Purim it's the

Persians; at Passover we hate Egypt, at Lag B'omer, Rome. On May Day we demonstrate against England; on the Ninth of Av we fast against Babylon and Rome; on the twentieth of Tammuz, Herzl and Bialik died, while on the eleventh of Adar we must remember for all eternity what the Arabs did to Trumpedor and his companions at Tel Hai. The Tree Planting festival is the only one where we haven't quarrelled with anyone and have no griefs to remember. But it almost always rains then—it does it on purpose."

My Uncle Zemach, they had explained to me, was Grandmother Emilia's eldest son by her first marriage, before she married Grandfather Isidore. Sometimes, when he was staying with us, Uncle Zemach would get me out of bed at half past five in the morning and incite me in a whisper to steal into the kitchen with him and cook ourselves an illicit double omelette. He would have a cheerful, even wicked gleam in his eye on those mornings, behaving just as if he and I were fellow members of some dangerous gang and only temporarily engaged in such a relatively innocent pastime as cooking ourselves illicit double omelettes. But my family generally had a very low opinion of my Uncle Zemach. Like this for instance:

"He was a little *spekulant** by the time he was fourteen in Warsaw, in the Nalevki district, and now here he is, still a *spekulant* in Bugrashov Street in Tel Aviv." Or:

---

*Black marketeer

"He hasn't changed an atom. Even the sun can't be bothered to brown him. That's the type he is. And there's nothing whatever we can do about it."

But I regarded that last remark as plain stupid and nasty, as well as unfair. My Uncle Zemach didn't get brown because he couldn't and that was all there was to it. Even if they'd made him a lifeguard on the beach he'd have got burnt instead of brown, turned red all over and begun to peel. This is how he was; a young man still, not tall, and so thin and pale he might have been cut out of paper. His hair was whitish, his eyes red like a rabbit's.

And what did *spekulant* mean anyway? I had no idea at all. But in my own mind I translated it more or less as follows:

That even when he lived in Warsaw, Uncle Zemach had used to wear a vest and khaki shorts down to his knees and fall fast asleep with the radio on. And he still had not changed; he still clung to his outlandish habits, wore a vest and khaki shorts down to his knees and fell asleep with the radio on. Even here, in Palestine, in Bugrashov Street, Tel Aviv. Well, I thought, what about it, so what?—what's wrong with that? And anyway, my Uncle Zemach lived in Grusenberg Street, not Bugrashov Street. And anyway, sometimes he would burst out singing very loudly in a voice that mooed and brayed and broke,

"Oh, show me the way to go home. . . ."

At which they would whisper together, very worried and in Yiddish so that I wouldn't understand, but always with the word *meshuggener,* which I knew meant madman. But though they said this of Uncle Zemach, he struck me rather—when he burst out with this song or any other—as not at all a mad man, but simply very sad.

And sometimes he wasn't sad either. Not at all: quite the reverse, he'd be joyous and funny. For instance, he would sit with my parents and my unmarried Aunt Edna on our balcony at dusk and discuss matters which ought not under any circumstances to have been discussed in front of children.

Bargains and profits, building lots and swindles, shares and *lirot,** scandals and adulteries in Bohemian circles. Sometimes, until they silenced him furiously, he used dirty language. "Quiet, Wetmark," they would say, "what's the matter with you, are you crazy, have you gone completely out of your mind? The boy's listening to everything and he's no baby any more."

And the presents he would bring me. He kept on thinking up the most amazing, even outrageous, presents. Once, he brought me a Chinese stamp album that twittered when you opened it. Once, a game like Monopoly, only in Turkish. Once, a black pistol that squirted water in your enemy's face. And once he brought me a little aquarium with a pair of live fish swimming about in it, except they were not a pair, as it turned out, but both indubitably male. Another time, he brought me a dart gun

---

*Pounds

("Are you out of your mind, Wetmark? The boy's going to put someone's eye out with that thing, God forbid"). And one winter weekend I got from Uncle Zemach a Nazi bank note—no other boy in our neighborhood had anything like it ("Now, Wetmark, this time you have really gone too far"). And, on Seder night, he presented me with six white mice in a cage ("So what else are you going to bring the boy? Snakes? Bedbugs? Cockroaches, perhaps?").

This time, Uncle Zemach marked the feast of Shavuot by riding all the way from the Egged bus station in the Jaffa Road to the courtyard of our house on a second-hand Raleigh bicycle, complete with every accessory: it had a bell, also a lamp, also a carrier, also a reflector at the back; all it lacked was the crossbar joining the saddle to the handlebars. But, in my first overwhelming joy, I overlooked just how grave a shortcoming that was.

Mother said: "Really, this is excessive, Zemach. The boy is still only eleven. What are you proposing to give him for his Bar Mitzva?"

"A camel," said Uncle Zemach at once, and with an air of such total indifference, he might have prepared himself for this very question all along.

Father said: "Would it be worth your considering at least once the effects on his education? Seriously, Zemach, where's it all leading to?"

I did not wait for Uncle Zemach's reply. Nor did it matter to me in the least where things were leading. Crazy with pride and joy, I was galloping my bicycle to my private place behind the house. And there, where no one could see me, I kissed its handlebars, then kissed the back of my own hands again and again and, in a whisper as loud as a shout, chanted: "Lord God Almighty, Lord God Almighty, LORD GOD ALMIGHTY." And, afterwards, in a deep, wild groan that broke from the depths of my being: "HI—MA—LA—YA."

And after that, I leaned the bicycle against a tree and leaped high into the air. It was only when I calmed down a little that I noticed Father. He stood in a window above my head and watched in unbroken silence until I had quite finished. Then he said:

"All right. So be it. All I beg is that we should make a little agreement between us. You may ride your new bicycle for up to an hour and a half each day. No more. You'll ride always on the right-hand side, whether there is traffic in the street or not. And you will remain always, exclusively, within the boundaries set by the following streets: Malachi, Zephania, Zachariah, Ovadia and Amos. You will not enter Geula Street, because it is too full of the comings and goings of the British drivers from the Schneller Barracks; whether they are intoxicated or the enemies of Israel, or both, is immaterial. And at all intersections you will kindly, please, use your intelligence a little."

"On the wings of eagles," said Uncle Zemach.

And Mother added: "Yes, but carefully."

I said: "Fine, good-bye." But when I had gone a little way from them, added: "It will be all right." And went out into the street.

How they stared at me then, the boys of our neighborhood; classmates, big boys, little boys alike. I watched them too, but sideways, so that they wouldn't notice it, and saw envy, mockery and malice there. But what did I care? Very slowly and deliberately I walked in front of them, not riding my bicycle, but pushing it, one-handed, along the pavement, right under their noses, wearing on my face meanwhile a thoughtful, even smug, expression, as if to ask:

"What's all the fuss about? It's just a Raleigh bicycle. Of course you can do exactly as you like. You can burst on the spot if you like, but it's your own lookout. It's got absolutely nothing to do with me."

Indeed, Elie Weingarten could not keep silence any longer. He opened his mouth and said, very coolly, like a scientist identifying some unusual lizard just discovered in a field:

"Just look at this. They've gone and bought Soumchi a girl's bike, without a crossbar."

"Perhaps they'll buy him a party frock next," said Bar-Kochba Sochobolski. He did not even bother to look at me, nor cease tossing deftly, up and down, two silver coins at once.

"A pink hair ribbon would suit Soumchi very well"—this was the voice of Tarzan Bamberger. "And he and Esthie can be best friends." (Bar-Kochba again.) "Except Esthie wears a bra already and Soumchi doesn't need one yet." (Elie Weingarten, the skunk.)

That was it. Enough, I decided. More than enough. Finish.

I did not start calling them names or set about breaking their bones one by one. Instead I made them the same rude gesture with my left thumb that Uncle Zemach made whenever the name of the British Foreign Minister, Bevin, was mentioned, turned around instantly and rode off on my bicycle down Zephania Street.

Let them say anything they liked.

Let them burst in a million pieces.

Why should I care?

Besides, on principle, I never pick a fight with boys weaker than myself. And, besides, what was all this about Esthie suddenly? What made them think of Esthie? Right then. It was still daylight. I would set off here and now on my bicycle for faraway places, head south on the Katamon and Talpiot Road, and on farther, via Bethlehem, Hebron and Beersheva, via the Negev and Sinai deserts, towards the heart of Africa and the source of the River Zambezi, there to brave alone a mob of bloodthirsty savages.

But I had barely reached the end of Zephania Street when I began to ask myself: Why do they hate me so, those bastards? And knew, suddenly, in my heart of hearts that it was my fault just as much as theirs. I felt an instant sense of relief. After all, an ability to show mercy even to his worst enemy is the mark of a great and noble soul. No power in all the world, no possible obstacle could deter such a man from traveling to the farthest frontiers of unknown lands. I would go now to consult Aldo, I decided, and afterwards, this very day and without more ado, would continue on my journey to Africa.

Who Shall Ascend unto the Hill of the Lord?

In which negotiations are concluded, a contract signed and a number of plans discussed, as are faraway places where no white man has ever set foot.

In the last house but one in Zephania Street lived my friend, Aldo Castelnuovo, whose father was famous for his conjuring tricks with matches and playing cards; besides which he owned a large travel agency, *The Orient Express.* I knew that Aldo, of all people, must see my new bicycle. It was the one thing his parents had not bought him, though they had bought him almost everything else. They would not allow Aldo a bicycle because of the various dangers involved and, in particular, because it might hinder Aldo's progress on the violin. It was for this reason that I whistled to Aldo furtively, from outside his house. When Aldo appeared he took the situation in at a glance, managing to smuggle the bicycle quickly into a disused shed in their back garden without his mother having suspected anything at all.

Afterwards, we both went into the house and shut ourselves up in Aldo's father's library (Professore Emilio Castelnuovo having gone to Cairo for four days on business). It greeted me, as usual, with a smell both gloomy and enticing, made up of muttered secrets and hushed carpets, stealthy plots and leather upholstery, illicit whisperings and distant journeys. All day long, all summer long, the library shutters were kept closed to prevent sunlight fading the beautiful leather bindings with their gold-lettered spines.

We took out the huge German Atlas and compared carefully every possible route on the map of Africa. Aldo's mother sent the Armenian nanny, Louisa, to us with a dish full of nuts—peanuts and almonds, walnuts and sunflower seeds—also orange juice in delicate blue glasses, still sweating with cold.

When we had demolished the peanuts and walnuts and begun on the sunflower seeds, the conversation turned to bicycles in general and my bicycle in particular. If Aldo were secretly to own a bicycle, it should be possible, we decided, to keep it hidden from all suspicious eyes, at the back of the disused shed. And then, early on Saturday mornings, while his parents were still safely fast asleep, he would be able to creep out; there would be nothing to stop him riding right to the end of the world.

I pronounced expert opinions on a thousand and one relevant items, approving or disapproving of them accordingly. On spokes and valves and safety valves; on batteries as compared to dynamos; on hand brakes (which, applied at speed, would send you flying immediately) as against back pedal brakes (let them go on a downhill slope and you might as well start saying your prayers); on ordinary carriers as compared to spring carriers; on lamps and reflectors, and so on and so forth. Afterwards, we returned to the subject of the Zulu and the Bushmen and the Hottentot, what each tribe had in common and in which way each one was unique, and which of them was the most dangerous. I spoke, eagerly, about the terrible Mahdi of Khartoum in the capital city of Sudan, about the real, original Tarzan from the forests of Tanganyika, through which I would have to pass on my journey to the source of the River Zambezi in the land of Obangi-Shari. But Aldo was not listening any more. He was miles away, deep in his own thoughts and seemed to grow more nervous every minute. Suddenly he cut me short, and, in a voice high and trembling with excitement, burst out:

"Come on! Come to my room: I'll show you something better than you've dreamed in all your life!"

"O.K. But quick," I begged. "I've got to get started on my journey today."

Yet, even so I followed him out of the library. To reach Aldo's room meant traversing almost the entire length of the Castelnuovos' house. It was very large, all its carpets and curtains spotlessly clean, yet contriving at one and the same time to be both faintly gloomy and a touch exotic. In the sitting room, for instance, there was a brown grandfather clock with golden hands and square Hebrew letters instead of numbers. There were low cupboards along the walls and on top of them rows and rows of small antiques made of wood or solid silver. There was even a silver crocodile, but its tail was no ordinary tail—it acted as a lever also. If you pulled it and then pressed very lightly the crocodile would crack nuts between its jaws for the benefit of the Castelnuovos' guests. Moreover, the door of the hallway between the drawing room and the oblong dining room was guarded balefully night and day by Caesario, a large woollen dog, stuffed with seaweed and glowering at you with black buttons in place of eyes.

In the dining room itself stood an enormous table made of mahogany, wearing what looked like felt stockings on each of its thick legs. And on the wall of the dining room in letters of gold, this inscription appeared: *Who shall ascend unto the hill of the Lord? Who shall stand in His holy place?* The answer to that question, *He who has clean hands and a pure heart*—which happened also to be the Castelnuovo family motto—was to be found on the opposite wall encircling the family crest; a single blue gazelle, each of its horns a Star of David.

From the dining room, a glass door led to a little cubbyhole called "The Smoking Room." An enormous painting hid one wall entirely. It showed a woman in a delicate muslin dress, a silk scarf concealing all her face except for her two black eyes, while, with one white hand, she held out to a beggar a golden coin so bright and shining it sprayed small sparks in all directions, like sparks from a fire. But the beggar himself continued to sit there peacefully. He wore a clean white cloak, his beard too was white, his eyes closed, his face radiant with happiness. Beneath the picture on a small copper plaque was engraved the single word *CHARITY*.

I marvelled so often in this house. At Louisa, for instance, the Armenian nanny who looked after Aldo; a dark and very polite girl of sixteen or seventeen whom I never saw without a clean white apron on top of her blue dress, both dress and apron looking newly ironed. She could talk Italian with Aldo, yet obeyed his order without question. She was also exceedingly courteous to me, calling me "the young gentleman," in a strange, almost dreamlike, Hebrew until sometimes, even to myself, I began to seem like a real young gentleman. Could she be the daughter of the woman in that great picture in the smoking room; and if not, why the likeness between them? And then, was *CHARITY* the name of the picture? Or the name of the woman in the picture? Or even the name of the painter who had painted it? Our teacher in Class Two had been called Margolit Charity. It was she who had given Aldo the Hebrew name "Alded." But who could give a name like Alded to a boy in whose house there was a room just for smoking?

(My parents' flat, with its two rooms and kitchen, separated by a short corridor, had only plain wooden tables and chairs with rush seats. Anemones or sprays of almond blossom flowered there in yoghourt jars in spring, while in summer and autumn the same jars sprouted branches of myrtle. The picture on the wall of the larger of our rooms showed a pioneer carrying a hoe and looking, for no obvious reason, towards a row of cypresses.)

At the far end of the smoking room was a strange low door. We went through it and down five steps to the wing of the house which contained Aldo's room. His window looked out on the crowded red roofs of the Mea Shearim quarter, and beyond them, eastwards, onto church towers and mountains.

"Now," said Aldo, as if about to perform some kind of magic, "now, just take a look at this."

And at that, he bent down and pulled from a large and brightly patterned box, section after section of dismantled railway track, several small stations and a railway official made of tin. There followed the most marvellous blue engine, with a quantity of red carriages. Then we lay down on the floor and began to put it all together, the track layout, the signaling system, even the scenery. (It too was made of brightly painted tin; hills and bridges, lakes and tunnels; tiny cows had even been painted on the hillsides, grazing peacefully alongside the steep track.)

And when at last all was ready, Aldo connected the electric plug and the whole enchanted world sprang instantly to life. Engines whistled, coach wheels clicked busily along the tracks, barriers went up and came down again, signal lights flashed intermittently at crossings and switches; freight trains and passenger trains, exchanging hoots of greeting, passed or overtook each other on parallel rails—magic upon magic, enchantment on enchantment.

"This," said Also with a slight disdain, "this I got as a present from my godfather, Maestro Enrico. He's Viceroy of Venezuela now." I was silent with awe.

But in my heart I was thinking:

Lord God Almighty. King of the Universe.

"As far as I am concerned," added Aldo with indifference, "the whole thing's pretty boring. Not to say a waste of time. Myself, I'd rather play my violin than play with toys these days. So you might as well have it. If you still play with toys, that is."

"Hallelujah, Hallelujah," my soul sang within my breast. But I still said nothing.

"Of course"—Aldo grew more precise—"of course, I don't mean as a present. As a swap. In exchange for your bicycle. Do you agree?"

Wow, I thought to myself. Wow. And how. But out loud, I said, "O.K. Done. Why not?"

"And of course," went on Aldo immediately, "of course I don't mean the whole thing. Just one section of it in exchange for your bike; one engine, that is, five carriages and three meters of circular track. After all, your bike doesn't have a crossbar. What I'm going to do now is fetch a blank contract from Father's drawer, and if you haven't had second thoughts and changed your mind—which you still have a perfect right to do—we can sign it there and then and shake hands on it. In the meantime, you may start choosing the amount of track and the number of carriages that we agreed, plus your one engine—one of the small ones of course, not the large. I'll be back in a minute. *Ciao.*"

But I was not listening any more. I couldn't hear anything except my own heart galloping away inside my breast and bellowing out: "Shoe — shoe — shoe — shoe — shoey-shoe" (which was a nonsense song absolutely everyone was singing in those days).

In a minute the contract had been signed and I had left the Castelnuovos' house, bursting out into Zephania Street like a train out of a tunnel, carrying carefully in front of me a shoe box gift-wrapped and tied up with blue ribbon. To judge by the light and the coolness of the air, it was half an hour or so till dusk and suppertime. I would set out the railway, I thought, in the wild and untamed landscape of our garden. I would dig a winding river, I thought, and fill it with water and make the railway cross it on a bridge. I'd raise hills and scoop out valleys, run a tunnel beneath the hanging roots of the fig tree and from there my new railway would erupt into the wilderness itself, into the barren Sahara and beyond, up to the source of the River Zambezi in the land of Obangi-Shari, through deserts and impenetrable forests where no white man had ever set foot.

Your Money or Your Life

In which we confront an old enemy, a bitter and cunning foe, who will stop at nothing. To avoid unnecessary bloodshed, we are obliged to fight our way through a thicket of intrigue and even to tame a young wild beast.

To judge from the fading light and cooler air, night and suppertime were approaching fast. At the corner of Jonah Street I stopped for a moment to read a new inscription on the wall. Two mornings ago it had been empty, but here now in black paint was a fierce slogan against the British and David Ben-Gurion. It was such a silly, irritating slogan in fact, even the spelling mistake seemed shocking.

British go hom
Get out Ben Gurion

I identified its author immediately. Goel. For this was no slogan from the Underground. This had to be the work of Goel Germanski himself. Having determined which, I took out a notebook and pencil and started to copy the inscription down. I need to make a note of everything like that, since I am going to be a poet when I grow up.

I was still standing there, writing, when Goel himself appeared. Large and silent, he crept up behind me, moving as precisely as a wolf in a forest. He grabbed my shoulders in his two strong hands and did not let me go. I did not struggle. For one thing, I don't, on principle, pick fights with boys stronger than myself. For another, I had not forgotten that I was clutching my railway, my dearest possession, in a box beneath my arm. Consequently, I needed to take particular care.

Goel Germanski was our class hoodlum, our neighborhood hoodlum, you could say. He was very tough and muscular, the son of the deputy headmaster of our school. His mother, it was rumored, "worked in Haifa for the French." Since our heavy defeat at Purim at the hands of the Bokarim quarter, we had been enemies, Goel and I. These days we did talk to each other, even went so far as to discuss our defeat, but always using the third person. And if I saw on Goel a certain ominous smile, I would do my best to be found on the opposite side of the street. For Goel's smile said this, approximately:

"Everyone except you knows that something very nasty is about to get you; any time now you'll know it too; all the rest of us will be laughing, only you will be laughing on the other side of your face."

Meanwhile, Goel had gripped my shoulders and asked, smiling, "So what's his little game then?"

"Please let me go," I begged politely. "It's late and I'm already supposed to be back home."

"Is that so then?" inquired Goel, letting go my shoulders. But he did not stop staring at me suspiciously, as if I had said something amazingly cunning; yet, if I had hoped thereby to fool Goel Germanski himself, then I had another think coming. That was how Goel looked at me.

Then he added very quietly:

"So he wants to go home, huh."

It was no question the way he said it. It was more as if he was pointing at some nasty aspect of my character which he was only just discovering, much to his sorrow and disappointment.

"I'm late already," I explained gently.

"Just get an earful of this," cried Goel to some invisible audience. "So he's late, huh? So all at once he wants to go home, huh? He's nothing but a dirty British spy, that's all he is. But as from right now we've got him fixed, him and his informing. As from right now we've fixed him for good."

"To start with," I corrected him cautiously, my heart

pounding under my T-shirt, "to start with, I'm not a spy."

"So he isn't is he?" winked Goel, simultaneously friendly and malevolent. "So how come he's copying that stuff from the wall, how come?"

"So what?" I inquired. And then, with a burst of courage, added: "The street doesn't belong to him. The street's public property."

"That's what he thinks," explained Goel, with a schoolmasterly patience, "that's what he thinks. Because right now he's going to start opening up that parcel of his and letting us take a good look inside."

"No I'm not."

"Open up."

"No."

"For the third and last time. He'll open up. If he knows what's good for him. That Soumchi. That scab. That dirty British spy. He'll open up, and fast, else I'll give him a hand right now."

So I untied the blue ribbon, removed the fine wrappings, revealed to Goel Germanski my railway, in all its glory.

After a brief, awed silence, Goel said, "And is he going to tell me he got all that from Sergeant Dunlop? Just for informing and nothing else?"

"I'm not an informer. I teach Sergeant Dunlop Hebrew sometimes and he teaches me English. That's all. I'm not an informer."

"Then how come the railway? How come the engine?

Unless, maybe, this well-known benefactor suddenly started handing out goodies to the poor?"

"It's none of his business," I said in the ensuing silence, heroically.

In return, Goel Germanski grabbed hold of my T-shirt and shook me against the fence, two or three times. He did not shake me savagely but delicately rather—I might have been a winter coat from which he was trying to remove dust and the smell of mothballs.

And when he had quite finished, he inquired anxiously, as though concerned for my welfare, "Maybe he's ready to do some talking now?"

"O.K.," I said. "O.K. O.K. If he'll let go of me. I swapped it. If he must know."

"He wouldn't be lying by any chance?" Goel sounded suspicious suddenly, wore on his face an expression of the deepest moral concern.

"Cross my heart. It's the absolute truth," I swore. "I swapped it with Aldo. There's even a contract in my pocket to prove it. Then he can see for himself. I swapped it for the bike I got from my uncle."

"Uncle Wetmark," Goel pointed out.

"Uncle Zemach," I corrected him.

"A girl's bike," said Goel.

"With a lamp and a dynamo," I insisted.

"Aldo Castelnuovo?" said Goel.

"As a swap," I said. "Here's the contract."

"Right," said Goel. And thereafter looked thoughtful.

We were silent for a little while. In the sky, and outside, in the courtyard, it was still daylight. But I could smell the evening approaching now. Goel broke the silence at last.

"Right," he said. "He's made one swap. Now here's another for him, if he wants. Psssst. Keeper. Here: down, sit! Sit! Right, like that. Good dog. Yes, you are. This is Keeper; he'd better take a good look at him before he makes up his mind. There's no dog like him today. Not even for fifty pounds apiece. They don't sell dogs with such pedigrees any more. His father belongs to King Farouk of Egypt; his mother to Esther Williams, in the pictures."

At Goel's shrill whistle and the sound of the name Keeper, a very young and enthusiastic Alsatian had sprung from the nearest courtyard and begun prancing all around us, panting and yelping and leaping and quivering, dancing with happiness, exploding with excitement, still so nearly a puppy he waggled his whole hindquarters, instead of just his tail. He fawned and fawned on Goel: he pressed himself against him, as if attempting to implant himself; begged his attention, to stay with him forever; flattered and beseeched him; clambered over him, his paws trembling with joy, his eyes firing sparks of wolfish love at him. In the end he was standing on his hind legs, scrabbling with all his might at Goel's stomach, until Goel checked him suddenly, with a masterful, "That's enough! Sit!"

In an instant, Keeper's lovemaking came to an abrupt

halt. His manner changed completely. He sat himself down, folding his tail neatly about him, expression thoughtful, even smug. He held his back, his head, his muzzle, as tense and still as if he were balancing a shilling on the end of his black nose. His furry ears were pricked. He was wrapped in such total gravity and humility, and he looked so like a newly-arrived immigrant boy, a particularly clean and tidy boy, trying his hardest to please, that it was almost impossible not to burst out laughing.

"Die," roared Goel, huskily.

Instantly Keeper prostrated himself at his feet and threw his head on his paws in eternal submission. His grief was as delicate as a poet's. His tail lay motionless, his ears were limp and totally despairing; he appeared to have ceased to breathe. Still, when Goel broke a small branch from a mulberry tree behind the fence, Keeper did not move; did not even blink an eye. And only the faintest of tremblings flowed along his back and made his grey-brown fur quiver.

But when, suddenly, Goel threw the stick into the distance and yelled "Fetch!" in a stern voice, the dog sprang, instantly—no, did not spring, erupted—like a shower of sparks out of a bonfire, parting the air, describing four or five wide arcs on it, as if he might in his fury have sprouted invisible wings. His wolf's jaw opened—I caught one brief glimpse of a red-black gullet, of white teeth sharpened for the kill—the next minute Keeper was back from his errand and laying the stick at his master's feet.

Then he too lay down in mute, even slavish submission, as if confessing that he was fit for nothing, so demanded nothing, except to fulfil his obligations, naturally, for what's one caress between you and me in the end?

"Well, that's it," said Goel.

While the dog lifted his head and looked up at him with eyes full of longing and barely concealed love, that asked:

"Am I a good dog then?"

"Yes," said Goel. "Yes, a very good dog. But you're going to change masters now. And if he doesn't treat Keeper well"—though Goel was addressing me now he still did not look at me—"if he doesn't treat Keeper well, I'll kill him on the spot. I'll kill him; get that, Soumchi?"

He spoke these last words in a menacing whisper, his face thrust close up to mine.

"Me?" I asked, hardly daring to believe my ears.

"Yes, him," said Goel. "He's getting Keeper, as from now. And then I'll know for sure he's not an informer."

The dog was still only a puppy, though no longer helpless and no longer little. He'll obey my voice, I thought. And how. And I'll turn him back into a proper wolf, a real fierce proper wolf.

"Has he ever read *The Hound of the Baskervilles*?" asked Goel.

"Of course I have," I said. "At least twice, if not three times."

"Good. Then he'd better know this dog's been trained to tear throats out too. British cops' and spies' throats. At a word of command. And that word's the name of the King of England—I won't say it now or he'll start attacking someone here."

"Of course," I said.

"And on top of that, he'll take messages anywhere he's sent. And track down a suspect just from sniffing at one of his socks," added Goel. And after a short silence, as if he was having to take a difficult and painful decision, muttered: "Right. O.K. He gets Keeper. In exchange, that is. As a swap. Not for free. For the railway."

"But . . ."

"And if he won't, I'll show the whole class the love poem he wrote Esthie Inbar in the black notebook Aldo stole from the pocket of his windbreaker in the Tel Arza wood."

"Bastards," I hissed, between gritted teeth. "Contemptible bastards." (Contemptible was a word I'd learned from Uncle Zemach.)

Goel found it expedient to ignore these epithets and preserve his good humor. "If he'll let me finish; before he starts swearing at me. Whatever that was all about. If he'll just let someone else say something. If he'll just keep his cool. He'll not only get Keeper in exchange, he'll get back his black notebook, and as well as that, he can join the Avengers, and as well as that I'll make peace with him. He only has to think a bit and he'll know what's good for him."

At that very moment a delicious haze spread through

my body. Excitement gently stroked my back; there was a melting in my throat and my knees were trembling with delight.

"Hang on," I protested, at the sight of Goel beginning to untie the blue ribbon from the railway box to improvise a lead for Keeper. "Hang on, hang on a minute."

"There you are, Soumchi." Goel actually addressed me in the second person as if we were friends again, as if nothing had happened at Purim in the battle with the Bokarim quarter, as if suddenly I was just like anybody else.

"There you are. Grab him. Only you've got to be firm with him. He might try and escape at first, until he gets used to you. Until he does, don't let him off the lead. In a few days he'll do just what you tell him. Just do me a personal favour, though, treat him properly. And tomorrow, at three o'clock, come to the secret place on Tarzan Bamberger's roof. On the stairs you'll have to tell Bar-Kochba the password, 'Lily of the Valley,' and wait for him to answer 'Rose of Sharon,' then you'll say 'Rivers of Egypt' and he'll let you past. Because those are the Avengers' passwords. And then you'll be sworn in and then you'll get your notebook back with those poems in I was talking about; I forget what they were about. Right. That's the lot. Just come tomorrow at three o'clock, or else. Go on, Keeper. Go with Soumchi. Go on, pull him, Soumchi. Pull him hard, like that. So long."

"So long, Goel," I answered, as if I really was just like

anybody else, though actually, inside my head, my soul went on singing over and over like some demented songbird, "I've got a wolf, I've got a wolf, I've got a young wolf to tear out throats." But it took all my strength to drag my reluctant wolf-cub after me. He dug his paws into the cracks in the pavement, protesting his wretchedness meanwhile with pathetic little whines that were beneath him altogether. So I ignored them. I just kept pulling him along. I pulled and walked and walked and pulled, while my spirit was borne far, far away, to the tangled forests and impenetrable jungles, where, surrounded, I made a brave and hopeless stand against a mob of shrieking cannibals, covered in war-paint and brandishing javelins and spears. Alone and weaponless, I struck out on all sides, but for every one of them I felled with my bare hands, a host of others swarmed yelling from their lair to take his place. Already my strength was beginning to fail. But then, as my enemies closed in on me with cries of joy, their white teeth gleaming, I gave one short, shrill whistle. From out of the thicket leaped my own private wolf, menacing, merciless, rending their throats with his cruel fangs until my enemies had scattered in all directions, bellowing with fear. Then he flung himself down at my feet and lay there panting, fawning on me and looking up at me with hidden love and longing, as if to say:

"Am I a good dog?"

"Yes, a very good dog," I said. But deep in my heart I

thought: This is happiness; and that's life. Here is love and here am I.

And, afterwards, darkness fell and we continued on our way through the gloom of the jungle to the source of the River Zambezi in the land of Obangi-Shari, where no white man had ever set foot, and to which my heart goes out.

To Hell with Everything

In which King Saul loses his father's asses and then finds a kingdom; and in which we too lose and find: and in which evening descends on Jerusalem and a fateful decision is reached.

The street was already darkening and it was growing late. Somehow I managed to drag the young wolf I got from Goel Germanski in exchange for an electric railway as far as the junction of Zephania and Malachi Streets. But there, just by the mailbox, set into the concrete wall, painted bright red, with a crown raised on it and underneath the initials, in English, of King George, the dog decided he had had enough. He pulled so hard, perhaps at the sound of some whistle I could not hear, he tore off the lead that Goel Germanski had made him out of the blue gift ribbon, so freeing himself. Then he crossed the road at a crouching run, his tail between his legs and his muzzle close to the ground, very furtive-looking, almost reptilian. Thereafter, he crept along, keeping his distance from me, as if admitting that such behaviour was disgraceful. Yet, claiming too, in his own defense:

"That's how it is, mate. That's life, I'm afraid."

And then he was gone from my sight altogether, vanished into the darkness of one of the courtyards.

Night fell.

And so that bad dog had returned quite certainly to his real master. And what was I left with? Just one small length of the blue ribbon that Aldo Castelnuovo had tied round the box that held the railway that Goel Germanski had converted into a lead for his dog. Otherwise, I was empty-handed, and also quite alone. But that was life.

By now, I had reached the courtyard of the Faithful Remnant Synagogue (which happened to be my short cut home, via the Bambergers' butcher shop). I did not hurry. I had no reason to hurry any more. On the contrary. I sat down on a box and listened to the sounds about me and began to set myself to thinking. Around and around flowed the warmth and peace of early evening. I heard the sound of radios from open windows, the sound of voices, laughing or scolding. Since it no longer mattered to anyone what would happen to me—not now or all the rest of my life—it did not matter much to me what would happen to anybody else. Yet, in spite of that, I felt sorry, at that moment, because everything in the world kept changing and nothing ever stayed the same, and sorry even that this evening would never come again, though I had no reason to love this evening. On the contrary, in fact. Yet I still felt sorry for what was and would not be a second time. And I wondered if there was some faraway place somewhere in the world, in Obangi-Shari perhaps, or among the Himalayan mountains, where it might be possible to order time not to keep on passing and light not to keep on changing, just as they had been ordered by Joshua, son of Nun in the Book of Joshua. At which, someone on one of the balconies called her neighbor a crazy fool and the neighbor answered for her part, "Just look who's talking. Mrs. Rotloi. Mrs. *Rotloi.*" And afterwards followed some gabbled, incomprehensible sentences, in Polish maybe. And suddenly a fearful shriek rose from Zachariah Street—for a moment I hoped that Red Indians had started to attack the neighborhood and were mercilessly scalping the inhabitants. But it was only a cat that cried and he only cried for love.

And among all the sounds of evening came the smells of evening; the smell of sauerkraut and tar and cooking oil, of souring garbage in garbage cans, and the smell of warm, wet washing hung out to catch the evening breeze. Because it was evening, in Jerusalem.

While I, for my part, sat on an empty box in the

courtyard of the Faithful Remnant Synagogue, wondering why I should keep trying to deny it all, about Esthie.

Esthie; who is, at this moment, quite certainly sitting in her room, which I'd never seen, nor was ever likely to. And equally certainly will have drawn her two blue curtains (with which, on the other hand, I was extremely well acquainted, having looked at them from the outside a thousand times and more). And is most probably doing the homework that I have forgotten to touch, answering in her round hand the simple questions set by Mr. Shitrit, the geography teacher. Or maybe untying her plaits, or rearranging them, or maybe, very patiently, cutting out decorations for the end-of-term party; her skirt stretched tightly across her lap; her nails clean and rounded, not black and split like mine. She is breathing very quietly—just as in class her lips will not quite be closed and every now and then she'll be trying to reach some imaginary speck on her upper lip with the tip of her tongue. I cannot tell what she is thinking about; except that certainly she is not thinking about me. And if something does happen to remind her of me, it is most likely as "that disgusting Soumchi"; or "that crazy boy." Better, therefore, she does not think of me at all.

And, anyway, that was quite enough of that. Better for me too to stop thinking about Esthie and instead start considering, very carefully, a much more urgent question.

I began to collect up my thoughts, just as my father had taught me to do at some moment of decision. He had taught me to set down on paper all possible courses of action, together with their pros and cons, erasing one by one the least promising of them, then grading the rest according to a point system. However, a pencil would be no use now, with daylight already gone. Instead, I listed the various alternatives in my head, as follows:

A. I could get up and go straight home, explaining my being late and empty-handed on the grounds that my bicycle had been stolen or else confiscated by some drunken British soldier, and I had not resisted him because my mother had ordered me not to argue with the soldiers, ever.

B. I could go back to Aldo's. Louisa, the Armenian nanny, would open the door to me and tell me to wait one moment. Then she would go by herself to announce that the young gentleman had returned and wanted a word with our young gentleman, and afterwards, very politely, she would usher me to the room where the magnificent lady in the muslin dress was presenting the beggar with a golden coin. And then I would have to confess to Aldo's mother that I had let Aldo have a bicycle, had even signed a contract for it. At which Aldo's mother would certainly punish him severely, because, under no circumstances, was he supposed to have a bicycle. And I would have behaved like a dirty low informer and not even got my bicycle back for my pains, since I no longer had the railway. Out of the question.

C. I could return to Goel Germanski. And announce in

a very cold and ominous voice that he was to return the railway immediately, our contract being cancelled. That he'd better give it back or I'd finish him for good. Yes, but how?

D. I could still return to Goel Germanski. But apparently friendly. "Hello, how are you, how's things?" And then ask casually if Keeper has come back to him by any chance? Yes. Of course. And tomorrow the joke will be all round the neighborhood. Total disgrace.

E. Who needs the wretched dog in any case? Who needs anything? I don't. So there. Anyway, who says Keeper fled straight back to Goel Germanski's? More likely he had run in the darkness to the Tel Arza wood and then on to the barren hills and then on to the forests of Galilee to join the rest of the pack in the wild and so to lead the life of a real free wolf at last, tearing out throats with his fangs.

Perhaps, right now, at this moment, I too could get to my feet and go to the Tel Arza wood; and from there to the hills and the caves and the winds to live as a bandit all the rest of my life and spread the fear of my name through the land forever.

Or, I could go home, tell, humbly, the whole truth, get my face slapped a few times and promise faithfully that from now on I would be a well-behaved and sensible boy instead of a crazy one. Then, straightaway, I would be dispatched with polite and apologetic notes from my father to Mrs. Castelnuovo and Mr. Germanski. I would apologize in my turn; assure everyone I hadn't really meant it;

would smile a stupid smile and beg everyone's pardon; tell everyone how sorry I was for everything that had happened. Quite out of the question.

F?G?H? Never mind. But a further possibility was simply to fall asleep among the ruins just like Huckleberry Finn in *The Adventures of Tom Sawyer*. I'd spend the night under the steps of the Inbars' house; in the very dead of night I'd climb the drainpipe to Esthie's room and we'd elope together to the land of Obangi-Shari before the crack of dawn.

But Esthie hates me. Perhaps worse than hates, she never thinks of me at all.

One last possibility. At Passover, I'd gone in Sergeant Dunlop's Jeep to an Arab village and never told my parents anything. Well now, I could go to Aunt Edna's in the Yegia Capiim neighborhood, look unhappy, tell her Father and Mother had gone to Beit Hakerem this morning to visit friends and wouldn't be back till late, so they'd left me a key, and, well, I didn't quite know how to put this, only, well, I seem to have lost it, and . . . But, oh, that Aunt Edna, who wore imitation fruit in her hair and had a house full of paper flowers and ornaments and never stopped kissing me and fussing over me . . . and . . . Never mind. It would have to do. At least it solved the problem for tonight. And by tomorrow Mother and Father would be so out of their minds with worry and so thankful to see me safe and well, they would quite forget to ask what had happened to my bicycle.

Right. Let's go. I got to my feet, having made up my

mind at last to beg shelter at my Aunt Edna's in the Yegia Capiim neighborhood. Only there was something glittering in the dark among the pine needles. I bent to the ground, straightened up again, and there it was, a pencil sharpener.

Not a large pencil sharpener. And not exactly new. Yet made of metal, painted silver, and heavy for its size, cool-feeling and pleasant to my hand. A pencil sharpener. That I could sharpen pencils with, but also make serve as a tank in the battles that I fought out with buttons on the carpet.

And so, I tightened my fingers round my pencil sharpener, turned and ran straight for home, because I wasn't empty-handed any more.

All Is Lost

"We'll never set foot . . ." In which I resolve to climb the Mountains of Moab and gaze upon the Himalayas, receive a surprising invitation (and determine not to open my hand, not as long as I shall live).

Father asked softly:

"Do you know what time it is?"

"Late," I said sadly. And gripped my pencil sharpener harder.

"The time is now seven thirty-six," Father pointed out. He stood, blocking the doorway, and nodded his head many times, as if he had reached that sad but inevitable conclusion there and then. He added: "We have already eaten."

"I'm sorry," I muttered, in a very small voice.

"We have not only eaten. We have washed up the dishes," revealed Father, quietly. There was another silence. I knew very well what was to follow. My heart beat and beat.

"And just where has his lordship been all this time? And just where is his bicycle?"

"My bicycle?" I said, dismayed. And the blood rushed from my face.

"The bicycle," repeated Father patiently, stressing each syllable precisely. "The bicycle."

"My bicycle," I muttered after him, stressing each syllable exactly as he did. "My bicycle. Yes. It's at my friend's house. I left it with one of my friends." And my lips went on whispering of their own accord, "Until tomorrow."

"Is that so?" returned Father sympathetically, as if he shared my suffering wholeheartedly and was about to offer me some plain but sound advice. "Perhaps I might be permitted to know the name and title of this honored friend?"

"That," I said, "that, I am unable to reveal."

"No?"

"No."

"Under no circumstance?"

"Under no circumstance."

It was now, I knew, he'd let fly with the first slap. I shrank right back, as if I was trying to bury my head between my shoulders, my whole body inside my shoes, shut my eyes and gripped my pencil sharpener with all my might. I took three or four breaths and waited. But no slap came. I opened my eyes and blinked. Father stood there, looking sorrowful, as if he was waiting for the performance to be over. At last he said,

"Just one more question. If his lordship will kindly permit."

"What?" my lips whispered by themselves.

"Perhaps I might be allowed to see what his excellency is concealing in his right hand?"

"Not possible," I whispered. But suddenly even the soles of my feet felt cold.

"Even this is not possible?"

"I can't, Daddy."

"His highness is showing us no favor today," Father summed up, sadly. Yet, despite everything, condescended to keep on pressing me: "For my benefit. And yours. For both our benefits."

"I can't."

"You will show me, you stupid child," roared Father. At that moment, my stomach began to hurt me dreadfully.

"I've got a tummy-ache," I said.

"First you're going to show me what you've got in your hand."

"Afterwards," I begged.

"All right," said Father, in a different tone of voice. And repeated suddenly, "All right. That's enough." And moved out of the doorway. I looked up at him, hoping above hope that he was going to forgive me after all. And in that very moment came the first of the slaps.

And the second. And afterwards the third. But, by then, I'd ducked out of the way of his hand and run outside into the street, running as hard as I could, bent low from sheer fright, just like Goel's dog when he ran away from me. I was in tears almost; in the process of making the dreadful decision: that I would shake the dust of that house from my feet for ever. And not just of the house; of the whole neighborhood, of Jerusalem. Now, at this moment, I'd set out on a journey from which I'd never return. Not for ever and ever.

So my journey began; but, instead of heading directly for Africa, as I'd planned earlier, I turned east, towards Geula Street, in the direction of Mea Shearim; from there I'd cross the Kidron Valley and follow the Mount of Olives road into the Judean Desert and thence to the Jordan crossing and thence to the Mountains of Moab, and on and on and on.

Ever since I was in Class Three or Four, my imagination had been captured by the Himalayan mountains, those sublime ranges at the heart of Asia. "There," I'd once read in an encyclopedia, "there, among them, rears the highest mountain in the world, its peak as yet unsullied by the foot of man." And there too, among those remote mountains, roamed that mysterious creature, the Abominable Snowman, scouring godforsaken ravines for his prey. The very words filled me with dread and enchantment:

ranges
  roams
    ravines
      remote
        sublime, unsullied,
                  eternal snows
                        and distant peaks.

And, above all, that marvellous word: Himalaya. On cold nights, lying beneath my warm winter blanket, I would repeat it over and over, in the deepest, most reverberant voice I could drag from the depths of my lungs. Hi — ma — la — ya.

If I could only climb to the heights of the Moab Mountains, I would look east and see far away the snow-capped peaks that were the Himalayas. And then, I would leave the land of Moab and travel south through the Arabian Desert, across the Gate of Tears to the coast of the Horn of Africa. And I would penetrate the heart of the jungle to the source of the River Zambezi, in the land of Obangi-Shari. And there, all alone, I'd live a life that was wild and free.

So, desperate, and burning with eagerness, I made my way east up Geula Street to the corner of Chancellor Street. But, when I reached Mr. Bialig's grocery, one thought overcame the rest; persistent, merciless, it repeated over and over. Crazy boy, crazy boy, crazy boy. Really you are crazy, stark raving mad, bad as Uncle Wetmark, maybe even worse; for all you know you'll grow up a *spekulant,* just like him. And what exactly did the word *spekulant* mean? I still did not know.

And suddenly all the pain and humiliation seemed to well up inside me, until I could scarcely bear it. The darkness was complete now in Geula Street. Not the darkness of early evening, full of children's cries and mothers' scoldings; this was the chill and silent darkness of the night, better seen from indoors, from your bed, through a crack in the shutters. You did not want to be caught out in it alone. Very occasionally someone else came hurrying by. Mrs. Soskin recognised me and asked what was the matter. But I did not answer her a word. From time to time a British armoured car from the Schneller Barracks charged past at a mad gallop. I would seek out Sergeant Dunlop, walking his poodle in Haturim Street or Tahkemoni Street, I thought, and this time I would give him information after all; I'd tell him it was Goel Germanski who painted that slogan against the High Commissioner. And then I would go to London and turn double agent. I'd kidnap the King of England and say to the English Government straight out: "Give us back the land of Israel and I'll give you back your King. Don't give, don't get." (And even this idea came from my Uncle Zemach.) There, sitting on the steps on Mr. Bialig's grocery, I rehearsed all the details of my plan. It was late now; the hour the heroes of the Underground emerged from their hiding places, while, around them, detectives and informers and tracker dogs lay in wait.

I was on my own. Aldo had taken my bicycle away and made me sign a contract to say so. Goel had expropriated my marvellous railway and the tame wolf roamed the woods and forests without me. And I was never to set foot in my parents' house again, not for ever and for ever. Esthie hated me. The despicable Aldo had stolen my notebook full of poems and sold it to that hoodlum Goel.

Then what was left? Just the pencil sharpener, nothing else. And what could I get from a pencil sharpener; what good could it do me? None. All the same, I'd keep it for ever and ever. I swore an oath that I would keep it, that no power on earth would take it from my hand.

So I sat at nine o'clock at night—or even at a quarter past nine—on the steps of Mr. Bialig's shuttered grocery shop and wept, almost. And so too I was found by a tall and taciturn man who came walking along the deserted street, smoking, peacefully, a pipe with a silver lid; Esthie's father, Mr. Engineer Inbar.

"Oh," he said, after he had leaned down and seen me. "Oh. It is you. Well, well. Is there anything I can do to help?"

It seemed beautiful to me, miraculous even, that Engineer Inbar should speak to me like that, as one adult to another, without a trace of that special kind of language and tone of voice that people use to children.

"Can I help you in any way?" I might have been a driver whose car had broken down, struggling to change a tire in the dark.

"Thanks," I said.

"What's the problem?" asked Engineer Inbar.

"Nothing," I said. "Everything's fine."

"But you're crying. Almost."

"No. No, not at all. I'm not crying. Almost. I'm just a bit cold. Honestly."

"All right. We're not going the same way by any chance? Are you on your way home too?"

"Well . . . I haven't got a home."

"How do you mean?"

"I mean . . . my parents are away in Tel Aviv. They're coming back tomorrow. They left me some food in the icebox. I mean . . . I had a key on a piece of white string."

"Well, well. I see. You've lost your key. And you've got nowhere to go. That's it in a nutshell. Exactly the same thing happened to me when I was still a student in Berlin. Come on then. Let's go. There's no point in sitting here all night, weeping. Almost."

"But . . . where are we going?"

"Home. Of course. To our place. You can stay the night with us. There's a sofa in the living room, also a camp bed somewhere. And I'm sure Esthie will be glad. Come on. Let's go."

And how my foolish heart ran wild; it beat inside my T-shirt, inside my vest, inside my skin and bone. Esthie will be glad—oh, Esthie will be glad.

Pomegranate scents waft to and fro
From the Dead Sea to Jericho.

Esthie will be glad.

I must never lose it; my pencil sharpener, my perfect, lucky pencil sharpener that I held in my hand that I held inside my pocket.

One Night of Love

How only he who has lost everything may sue for happiness.
"If a man offered for love all the wealth of his house . . ."
And how we were not ashamed.

So there we sat at supper together, Engineer Inbar and I, discussing the state of the country. Esthie's elder brother was away building a new kibbutz at Beit she'an, while her mother must have eaten before we came. Now she set before us on a wooden dish slices of some peculiar bread, very black and strong-tasting, together with Arab cheese, very salty, and scattered with little cubes of garlic. I was hungry. Afterwards we ate whole radishes, red outside, white and juicy inside. We chewed big lettuce leaves. We drank warm goat's milk. (At our house, that is to say the house that used to be mine, I'd get a poached egg in the evening, with tomato and cucumber, or else boiled fish, and afterwards yoghourt and cocoa. My father and mother ate the same, except they finished up with tea instead of cocoa.)

Mrs. Inbar gathered up the plates and cups and went back to the kitchen to prepare lunch for the next day. "Now we'll leave the men to talk men's talk," she said. Mr. Engineer Inbar pulled off his shoes and put his feet up on a small stool. He lit his pipe carefully, and said, "Yes. Very good."

And I tightened my fingers round the pencil sharpener in my pocket and said, "Thank you very much."

And afterwards we exchanged opinions on matters of politics. Him in his armchair; me on the sofa.

The light came from a lamp the shape of a street lamp on a copper column, which stood in one corner beside the desk and between one wall covered in books and maps and another hung with pipes and mementoes. A huge globe stood in the room too, on a pedestal. At the slightest touch of a finger I thought it could be made to spin round and round. I could hardly take my eyes off it.

All this time Esthie remained in the bathroom. She did not come out. There was only the sound of running water sometimes from behind the locked door at the end of the corridor, and sometimes, also, Esthie's voice singing one of the popular songs of Shoshana Damari.

"The Bible," said Engineer Inbar amid his cloud of smoke, "the Bible, quite right, no doubt, of course. The Bible promises us the whole land. But the Bible was written at one period, whereas we live in quite another."

"So what?" I cried, politely furious. "It makes no difference. Perhaps the Arabs called themselves Jebusites or Canaanites in those days, and the British were called Philistines. But so what? Our enemies may keep changing their masks, but they keep persecuting us just the same. All our festivals prove it. The same enemies. The same wars. On and on, almost without a break."

Engineer Inbar was in no hurry to reply. He grasped his pipe and scratched the back of his neck with the stem. And afterwards, as if he found an answer difficult, he began gathering up from the table every stray crumb of tobacco and impounding them carefully in the ash tray. When the operation was complete, he raised his voice and called:

"Esther! Perhaps it's time you made harbour and came to see who's waiting for you here. Yes. A visitor. A surprise. No, I'm not going to tell you who it is. Come to dry land quickly and you'll see for yourself. Yes. The Arabs and British. Certainly. Canaanites and Philistines, from the day that they were born. A very intriguing idea. Only you'll have to try to persuade them to see matters in the same light. The days of the Bible, alas, are over and done with. Ours are a different matter altogether. Who on earth nowadays can turn walking sticks into crocodiles and beat rocks to make water come out? Look, I brought these sweets back last week, straight from Beirut, by train. Try one. Go on. Enjoy it. Don't be afraid. It's called *Rakhat Lokoom.** Eat up. Isn't it sweet and tasty? And you—I assume you belong to some political party already?"

"Me? Yes," I stammered. "But not like Father . . . the opposite . . ."

"Then you support the activities of the Underground absolutely and resist any suggestion of compromise," stated Engineer Inbar, without a question mark. "Very good. Then we are of different minds. By the way, your school satchel, with all your books and exercise books must be locked up at home in your flat. That's a pity. You'll have to go to school tomorrow with Esthie, but without your satchel. Esther! Have you drowned in there? Perhaps we'd better throw you a life-belt or something."

"Please could I have another piece?" I asked politely; and boldly, not waiting for a reply, pulled nearer to me the jar of *Rakhat Lokoom.* It really was delicious, even if it did come straight from the city of Beirut.

It was so good to sit here in this room, behind closed shutters, and between the walls covered in books and maps and the wall hung with pipes and mementoes,

---

*Turkish Delight

immersed in frank men's talk with Engineer Inbar. It seemed miraculous that Engineer Inbar did not snub or ridicule me, did not talk down, merely remarked, "Then we are of different minds"—how I loved that expression, "We are of different minds." And I loved Esthie's father almost as much as I loved Esthie, only in a different way; perhaps I loved him more. It began to seem possible to open my heart and confess just how badly I'd lied to him; to make a clean breast of today's shame and disgrace, not even keeping from him where I was journeying to and the roads I intended to take. But, just then, at last, Esthie emerged from the bathroom. I almost regretted it—this interruption to our frank men's talk. Her hair was not in its plaits now—instead, there fell to her shoulders a newly-washed blonde mane, still warm and damp, still almost steaming. And she wore pyjamas with elephants all over them, large and small ones in different colors; on her feet her mother's slippers, much too big for her. She threw a quick glance at me as she came in, then went straight over to where her father, Engineer Inbar, was sitting. I might have been yesterday's newspapers left lying on the sofa; or else I stopped there every evening on my way to the land of Obangi-Shari; there was nothing whatever in it.

"Did you go to Jericho today?" Esthie asked her father.

"I did."

"Did you buy me what I asked?"

"I didn't."

"It was too expensive?"

"That's right."

"Will you look again for me when you're in Bethlehem next?"

"Yes."

"And was it you brought him here?"

"Yes."

"What's it all about then? What's up with him?"

(I still didn't merit one word, one glance from Esthie. So I kept silent.)

"His parents are away and he lost his key. Exactly the same thing happened to me when I was a student in Berlin. We bumped into each other on Geula Street and I suggested he come to us. Mama has already given him something to eat. He can spend the night on the sofa in the living room, or else on the camp bed, in your room. It's up to you."

Now, all at once, suddenly, Esthie turned towards me. But still without looking at me directly.

"Do you want to sleep in my room? Will you promise to tell me crazy stories before we go to sleep?"

"Don't mind," muttered my lips, quite of their own volition because I was still too stunned.

"What did he say?" Esthie asked her father a little anxiously. "Perhaps you heard what he said?"

"It seemed to me," answered Engineer Inbar, "it seemed to me that he was still weighing up the possibilities."

"Weighing-schneighing." Esthie laughed. "O.K., that's

it, let him sleep in here, in the living room and be done with it. Good night."

"But Esthie," I succeeded in saying at last, if still in a whisper only. "But Esthie . . ."

"Good night," said Esthie, and went out past me in her cotton elephant pyjamas, the smell of her damp hair lingering behind her. "Good night, Daddy."

And from outside, in the passage, she said, "Good. My room then. I don't mind."

Who ever, before, saw a girl's room, late, towards bedtime, when the only light burns beside her bed? Oh yes, even a girl's room has walls and windows, a floor and a ceiling, furniture and a door. That's a fact. And yet, for all that, it feels like a foreign country, utterly other and strange, its inhabitants not like us in any way. For instance: there are no cartridge cases on the windowsill, no muddy gym shoes buried under the bed. No piles of rope, metal, horseshoes, dusty books, pistol caps, padlocks and India rubber bands; no spinning tops, no strips of film. Nor are there subversive pamphlets from the Underground hidden between the cupboard and the wall and, presumably, no dirty pictures concealed among the pages of her geography book. And there aren't, wouldn't ever be, in a girl's room, any empty beer cans, cats' skulls, screwdrivers, nails, springs and cogs and hands from dismantled watches, penknife blades, or drawings of blazing battleships pinned up along the wall.

On the contrary.

In Esthie's room, the light was almost a color in itself; warm, russet-colored light, from the bedside lamp under its red raffia lampshade. Drawn across its two windows were the blue curtains that I'd seen a thousand times from the other side, and never dreamed I'd see from this, all the days of my life. On the floor was a small mat made of plaited straw. There was a white cupboard with two brown drawers in it, and, in the shadowy gap between wall and cupboard, a small, very tidy desk on which I could see Esthie's school books, pencils and paint-box. A low bed, already turned down for sleep, stood between the two windows; a folded counterpane, the color of red wine, at its head. Another camp bed had been placed ready for me, as close as possible to the door.

In one corner, on a stool covered with a cloth, there nestled a tall jug filled with pine branches and a stork made out of a pine cone and chips of colored wood. There were two more chairs in the room. One of them I could scarcely take my eyes off. But the bedside lamp bestowed its quiet light on everything alike. Russet-colored light. You are in a girl's room, I thought. In Esthie's room, I thought. And you just sit and don't say anything because you are just a great big dummy. That sums it up, Soumchi, absolutely sums it up. Which thought is not going to help me find the right words for starting a conversation. With much agony, I managed to squeeze out the following sentence, more or less:

"My room, at home, is quite different from this."

Esthie said, "Of course. But now you're here, not there."

"Yes," I said, because it was true.

"What do you keep staring at all the time?" asked Esthie.

"Nothing in particular," I said. "I'm just sitting here . . . just sitting. Not looking at anything in particular." That, of course, was a lie. I could scarcely take my eyes off the arms of the second chair on which she'd laid the beloved white jumper, the very same jumper that, at school, I'd stuck time and again to the seat of her chair with chewing gum. Oh, God, I thought. Oh, God, why did you make me such an idiot? Why was I ever born? At this moment it would be better not to exist. Not anywhere. Not anywhere at all, except perhaps in the Himalaya mountains or the land of Obangi-Shari, and even there they don't need such an idiot as me.

And so it was, after scraping those few words together, I sat dumb again on the folding bed in Esthie's room, my right hand still gripped tightly round my pencil sharpener and sweating a little in my pocket.

Esthie said, "Perhaps, after all, you'd rather sleep in the living room."

"It doesn't matter," I whispered.

"What doesn't matter?"

"Nothing. Really."

"O.K. If that's what you want. I'm getting into bed now and I'm going to turn round to the wall until you've got yourself quite settled."

But I did not think of settling myself quite. Still fully dressed in my very short gym shorts and Hasmonean T-shirt, I lay under the light blanket, taking nothing off but my gym shoes, which I threw as deep as possible beneath the bed.

"That's it. All clear."

"If you want, now you can tell me about the mutiny of the great Mahdi in the Sudan, just like you did to Ra'anana and Nourit and all the rest of them the day Mr. Shitrit was ill and we had two free periods."

"But you didn't want to listen then."

"But now is not then. It's now," Esthie pointed out quite correctly.

"And if you didn't listen to the story, how do you know that it was about the rebellion of the Mahdi in the Sudan?"

"I do know. Generally I know everything."

"Everything?"

"Everything about you. Perhaps even the things you think I don't know."

"But there's one thing you don't know and I won't ever tell you," I said, very quickly, in one breath and with my face to the wall and my back to Esthie.

"I do know."

"You don't."

"Yes."

"No."

"Yes."

"Then tell me and we'll see."

"No."

"That means you're only saying you know. You don't know anything."

"I know. And how."

"Then tell me. Now. And I swear I'll tell you if you're right."

"You won't tell."

"I swear I'll tell."

"Good then. It's this. That you love some girl in our class."

"That's rubbish. Absolutely."

"And you wrote her a love poem."

"You're nuts. You're mad. Stop it!"

"In a black notebook."

I would steal a thermometer from the medicine cabinet, I decided there and then. And I would break it. And, at the ten o'clock break, I'd let the mercury run out and mix a little of it with Aldo's cocoa and a little with Goel Germanski's. So that they'd die. And also Bar-Kochba's and Elie's and Tarzan Bamberger's. So that they'll all be dead, once and for all.

Esthie repeated:

"In a little black notebook. Love poems. And also poems about how you'd run away with this girl to the Himalaya mountains, or some place in Africa—I forget the name."

"Shut up, Esthie. Or I'll throttle you. This minute here. That's enough."

"Don't you love her any more?"

"But it's all lies, Esthie. It's all lies invented by those bastards. I don't love any girl."

"Good," said Esthie, and all at once turned out her bedside light. "That's O.K. If that's how you want it. Now go to sleep. I don't love you either."

And afterwards, while the street light slid through the cracks in the shutters and painted the room with stripes, on the table and on the chairs, on the cupboard and on the floor, on Esthie herself in her elephant pyjamas, lying at the other end of the straw mat at the foot of my bed, we talked a little more. In a whisper, I confessed almost everything. About Uncle Zemach and me; about how I was like him, a crazy boy, and for all anyone knew, a *spekulant* too in the end; about what it felt like to get up and leave everything, to go in search of the source of the River Zambezi in the land of Obangi-Shari. About how I'd left all of it, the house, the neighborhood, the city, and how, in one day, I'd managed to lose a bicycle, an electric railway, a dog and even my own home. How I'd been left without anything, except the pencil sharpener I found. Till late, very late at night, perhaps about eleven o'clock, I went on whispering to Esthie and she listened to me without a single word. But then, during the silence that fell, when I'd finished my story, she said, very suddenly:

"Good. Now give me this pencil sharpener."

"The pencil sharpener? Why give you the pencil sharpener?"

"Never mind. Give it me."

"Here you are then. Will you love me now?"

"No. And now be quiet."

"Then why are you touching my knee?"

"Will you be quiet. Why does he always have to say things and make trouble? Don't say any more."

"O.K." I said. But was forced to add, "Esthie."

Esthie said, "Enough. Don't say another word. I'm going away now to sleep on the sofa in the living room. Don't say anything. And don't say anything tomorrow either. Good night. And anyway, there's no such place as the land of Obangi-Shari. But it's marvellous all the same that you've invented a place for just us two alone. Goodbye, then, till tomorrow."

For six weeks Esthie and I were friends. All those days were blue and warm and the nights were blue and dark. It was full, deep summer in Jerusalem while we loved each other, Esthie and I.

To the end of the school year, our love continued, and a little after, over the summer holidays. What names our class called us, what stories they told, what a joke they found it. But all the time we loved each other, nothing could worry us. Then our friendship was over and we parted, I won't say on account of what. Haven't I already written, in the prologue, how time keeps on passing and that the whole world changes? In fact, this brings me to the end of my story. In a single sentence I can tell you all of it. How once I was given a bicycle and swapped it for a railway; got a dog instead; found a pencil sharpener in place of the dog and gave the pencil sharpener away for love. And even this is not quite the truth, because the love was there all the time, before I gave the sharpener away, before these exchangings began.

Why did love cease? That is just one question. But there are many other questions I could ask if I wanted. Why did that summer pass, and the summer after? And another summer and another and another? Why did Engineer Inbar fall ill? Why does everything change in the world? And why, since we happen to be asking questions, why, now that I'm grown up, am I still here and not among the Himalaya mountains and not in the land of Obangi-Shari?

Well then; but there are so many questions and among them some so very hard to answer. But, as for me, I've reached the end of my story—so, if anyone else can provide us with the answers, let him rise to his feet and give them to us now.

EPILOGUE

All's Well That Ends Well

Which may be skipped altogether.

I only wrote it because it is expected.

At midnight, or perhaps just after midnight, Mother and Father arrived at the Inbar family house, looking pale and frightened. Father had been searching for me since half past nine. First he had gone to inquire for me at my Aunt Edna's in the Yegia Capiim neighborhood. Then he had returned to our own neighborhood and inquired equally vainly at Bar Kochba's and Elie Weingarten's. At a quarter past ten he had arrived at Goel Germanski's; they had waked up Goel and interrogated him closely, Goel claiming that he knew absolutely nothing. By which Father's suspicions had been aroused; he had cross-examined Goel briefly himself, and, in the course of that, the agitated Goel swore several times that the dog did belong to him and that he even had a licence from the city council to prove it. Father had dismissed him at last, saying "We are going to have another little chat some time, you and I," and continued his search through the neighborhood. But it was nearly midnight before he learned from Mrs. Soskin that I had been seen sitting on the steps of Mr. Bialig's grocery, in tears, almost, and that half an hour later, Mrs. Soskin had happened to peer through her north-facing shutter and seen me still sitting there, and then, "All of a sudden, Mr. Engineer Inbar had appeared and enticed the boy away with him, by kind words and promises."

His face very white, his voice very low and quiet, Father said:

"So, here's our jewel at last; asleep in his clothes, the crazy boy. Get up please, and kindly put on your sweater that your mother has been toting round for you all evening from house to house till twelve o'clock at night. We'll go straight home now, and leave all accounts to be settled tomorrow. Forward march!"

He made polite apologies to Engineer Inbar and his

wife, thanked them and begged them in the morning to thank dear Esther also (whom, as we departed, I saw briefly a long way off through the open living-room door. She was tossing from side to side in her sleep, disturbed by the voices and murmuring something, probably that it was all her fault and they should not punish me. But no one besides me heard and I did not really).

Back in my bed, at home, I lay all night awake and bright and happy until the crack of day. I did not sleep. I did not want to sleep. I saw the moon depart from my window and the first line of light start gleaming in the east. And, at last, the sun setting early sparkles on drain-pipes and windowpanes, I said out loud, almost:

"Good morning, Esthie."

And indeed a new day was beginning. At breakfast, Father said to Mother, "All right. As you want. Let him grow up a Wetmark. I'll just keep my mouth shut."

Mother said, "If it's all the same to you, my brother's name is Zemach, not Wetmark."

Father said, "That's all right by me. Good. So be it."

At school, by the ten o'clock break, this had already appeared on the blackboard:

In the midnight, under the moon
Soumchi and Esthie start to spoon.

And the teacher, Mr. Shitrit, wiped it all off with a duster and calmly implored as follows:

"Not a dog shall bark. Let all flesh be silent."

On his return from work on that same day, at five o'clock, the turn of the evening, Father went alone to the Germanskis' house. He explained; apologized; made frank and complete statement of the facts; took possession of the electric railway and turned his footsteps, steadily and without haste, to the house of the Castelnuovo family. There, Louisa, the Armenian nanny, ushered him into Professor Castelnuovo's aromatic library and Father made an impartial statement of the facts to Mrs. Castelnuovo in her turn. He apologized; received apologies; handed over the railway and took possession of the bicycle. And so, at last, everything was restored to its rightful place once more.

The bicycle itself, of course, was confiscated and locked up in the cellar for three months. But I have already written how, by the end of the summer, everything had changed; how nothing stayed the same as before. How other concerns took over. But they, perhaps, belong to some other story.